Revenge of the Fireflies

J.B. Stamper

SCHOLASTIC INC.

New York Toronto London Auckland Sydney
Mexico City New Delhi Hong Kong Buenos Aires

**Cover illustration by
Marc Gabbana**

**Interior illustrations by
Greg Follender**

4 5 6 7 8 9 10   23   12 11 10 09 08 07

Contents

It's the year 2087. And somewhere in the universe, a spaceship is lost. . . .

1 Life Signs

Gwyn sat at the spaceship's control deck. She wrote in her captain's record book.

Date: July 22, 2087. It's the first day of **Mission** *X463. We've found no sign of the missing spaceship. . . .*

"Captain!" a voice behind her shouted. "I'm picking up signs of life!"

Gwyn jerked her head around. Carlos came rushing over. He was the head of mission science.

"Captain, look at this," he said. Gwyn read his **printout.** It showed a planet straight ahead. Signals were coming from the planet. They were signs of human life!

"We've found them," Gwyn said. "They're still alive!"

Gwyn's mission was to find a missing spaceship. The spaceship and its **crew** had disappeared three weeks ago. Until now, there had been no clues.

Pango ran up to the deck. He was the spaceship's **second-in-command**.

"Captain, there's a planet out there that's giving off a weird light. We have to change course. We don't want to hit it."

Gwyn turned quickly. She looked out over the control deck. There it was. The planet was big, and it was glowing.

"No, Pango," she said. "We're staying on course. The missing crew may be on that planet. We have to save them."

"If you say so," Pango said.

Pango sounded mad. He had lots of space experience. Gwyn didn't. But she was the leader of this mission. And she had made her decision.

Gwyn pointed the spaceship toward the planet. Carlos and Pango stood behind her. Everyone stared at the planet's strange light.

"Captain," Pango warned. "I've never seen anything like this. We have to turn around. It could be dangerous!"

Gwyn didn't listen to him. She kept her eyes on the planet. The bright light burned her eyes. She felt dizzy. Suddenly, everything went blank. She let go of the controls.

"We're going to crash!" Pango screamed.

Carlos grabbed the controls. He was just in time. The huge spaceship stopped. It floated just above the planet's surface.

Gwyn rubbed her eyes. She took a deep breath. She felt a little better.

"Are you okay, captain?" Carlos asked.

"Yes. Thank you, Carlos," she said. "I'm in control now."

Gwyn set the spaceship's controls to "**descend**." Her hands were shaking. The spaceship started to land. It got closer and closer to the surface of the planet.

The control panel began to beep. The countdown to landing began. *Ten, nine, eight, seven, six . . .*

Five, four, three, two, one. Touchdown.

The spaceship landed safely. Then the crew heard an ugly, crunching sound. It came from beneath them. It sounded like something being crushed *to death!*

Why did Gwyn ignore Pango's warning? Did she do the right thing?

Will Gwyn find the missing spaceship?
Or will she die trying?

2 Glowing Ooze

The spaceship began to shake. Something was moving under it. The crew crashed against the walls. And they fell on the floor.

Then they heard something under the spaceship. It was a horrible sound. Gwyn looked at her crew. Their faces were filled with fear.

Pango rushed to the window. "The light," he whispered. "It's gone!"

Everyone crowded around their captain. The planet was dark. But a green glow was coming from below the spaceship.

Gwyn faced her crew.

"I need six of you to come with me," she said. "We need to find the missing crew and bring them home."

Gwyn led the way out of the spaceship. Pango, Carlos, and four others followed her. They stepped out onto the planet. Their boots sank into soft **slime**.

Carlos saw the creature first. He gasped in terror. Everyone ran to see what it was.

At first, they only saw green **ooze**. It was spreading out from under the spaceship. And it was glowing.

"What is it?" Gwyn asked.

Six long, skinny legs stuck out from the slime. One leg was still moving.

Gwyn walked around to the front of the spaceship. Something was stuck between the spaceship and the slime. It was a huge, crushed **insect**! Its giant **antennas** reached out. They were as thick as whips.

"This . . . thing . . . has to be dead," she said to Carlos. "We landed right on top of it. But what is it?"

They looked closer. The slime coming out of the creature gave off an **eerie** glow.

Gwyn pulled on her safety gloves. She reached out and touched the slime.

"It reminds me of something on earth," Gwyn said.

"A firefly," Carlos said. "It's a huge firefly!"

The crew stared at the giant bug. They stood in silence. Pango was the first to speak.

"There was a mission many years ago," said Pango. "It was a mission to study fireflies. A **chemical** exploded on the spaceship. The crew all died. Some of the fireflies must have survived."

"And grown!" said Carlos.

"And here they are," Gwyn said.

"But that was a long time ago," Carlos said. "What about the people we're looking for now? They disappeared three weeks ago. We've picked up signs of human life on this planet. That crew must be around here somewhere!"

"We'll find them," Gwyn said. She turned on her **laser** light. She pointed it into the darkness.

The crew followed Gwyn. She turned her laser light to the left, to the right, and then behind them.

Gwyn thought she saw something. She took a step forward. Whatever it was disappeared.

"Step back," Carlos said. "Shine your laser where it was before."

Gwyn pointed her laser light back into the darkness. Something out there flashed again.

"It's a **reflection**," she said. "It looks like glass."

They all walked forward slowly.

A young crew member saw the jar first. She let out a scream that echoed across the planet.

Gwyn stared at the huge jar. Faces stared back at her from inside the jar. They were scared, human faces. Their hands were pressed up against the glass.

"It's . . . it's horrible!" Carlos said. "They're trapped! They're trapped in that glass jar like . . ."

Gwyn finished his thought.

"Like fireflies!" she said.

How do you think these people got stuck in the jar?

On earth, fireflies are harmless. On this planet, they're not!

The Survivors

The crew crowded around the huge glass jar. They stared at the humans trapped inside.

"There are only five people in there," Gwyn said. "But their spaceship had a crew of 20. Where are the others?"

"Maybe these are the only **survivors**," Pango said.

"How can we get them out of there?" someone asked.

"We'll push the jar on its side," Gwyn said. "Then we'll cut through the metal top. We'll use our lasers."

Gwyn tried to calm the scared men and

women inside the jar. Then her crew pushed the jar on its side. The planet's soft, slimy surface kept it from breaking.

Two crew members cut open the lid.

They pulled the five trapped humans from their big glass jar.

A young man was the first one out.

"Where is the rest of your crew?" Gwyn asked him.

"We're the only ones left," he said. "The insects picked us up out of our crashed spaceship. They put us in these jars."

A woman crawled out of the jar. Then she began to scream.

"Not again!" she screamed. "They're coming back for us!"

Gwyn looked up. She saw a mountain. Behind it, a light was glowing on and off.

Seconds later, the dark shapes of giant fireflies covered the mountain. Their **flickering** lights glowed brighter

and brighter in the sky.

"Everyone, run!" Pango screamed. "Run for the spaceship!"

But it was too late.

A firefly had come up behind them. Its huge body stood between them and their spaceship.

"There's a cave over there," a survivor gasped. "We've got to run for it."

Gwyn saw the cave. "Follow me!" she yelled. She grabbed one of the survivors. She pulled her to the cave.

Inside the cave, Gwyn found a huge rock.

"Roll it over the opening!" she ordered.

The crew began to push the rock. They could see the fireflies' lights getting brighter outside. They could hear their wings beating louder and louder.

Is there a way out of the cave? Or are Gwyn and the others trapped?

4 Caught!

The crew rolled the rock toward the opening. Just then, a giant firefly landed at the opening of the cave. Its eyes were huge. The crew saw their faces reflected in the insect's huge eyes.

"Get back!" Gwyn shouted at the huge insect. The firefly was reaching its front legs out to grab at them.

A second later, the crew rolled the rock into the cave's opening. The rock crushed the insect. The firefly's body broke in two. But its long antennas were whipping around. They hit Gwyn.

Pango rushed up to grab Gwyn's arm.

"Listen to that!" he whispered. He pointed up at the ceiling.

More and more fireflies were landing outside. The noise from their wings grew louder. It was like the sound of a **tornado**. Gwyn turned to her crew. She turned to the survivors they had saved. They were all terrified.

"There must be hundreds of them," a crew member said.

"No, thousands!" said a survivor.

"Do you hear that?" someone asked. "They're chewing at the stone. They'll chew at it until they get to us!"

Gwyn knew she had to take control. Everyone was about to panic.

"Carlos, find out what you can about fireflies. Everyone else, check every inch of this cave. There must be another way out of here!"

The crew spread out. They used their laser lights to search the cave. Carlos worked on his computer.

"Fireflies are part of the **beetle** family," he read on his computer screen. "They have two sets of wings. Only the second set is used for flying. Their light comes from some kind of **chemical reaction**."

"What do they eat?" Gwyn asked.

"Snails and earthworms," Carlos said. "First, they kill them with poison."

Outside, the sound of chewing grew louder and louder.

"We've got to get out of here!" Carlos yelled. "They're getting closer! Any second now, they'll chew through. They'll get in!"

Gwyn took the computer from Carlos. She read the report on fireflies. She read about where they lived. She learned how they found **mates**. She began to understand how they used their lights as signals.

"Carlos, look at that firefly," Gwyn said. "Tell me what kind it is."

Carlos knelt over the crushed firefly. *"Photinus pyralis,"* he said.

Gwyn heard his answer. But she didn't say anything at first. She just stared at the rock covering the cave door.

A small hole had opened up. And a hairy leg was wiggling through.

"Carlos," she screamed. "Get back!"

A giant firefly had chewed through the rock. It started taking big bites of rock. The hole it made got bigger. Soon, it would be able to get inside the cave!

Why did Gwyn want to learn about fireflies? How could this information help her?

More giant bugs are attacking. Is this the end for Gwyn and her crew?

5 Run for Your Life!

Carlos jumped to his feet. He and Gwyn ran deep into the cave.

Pango and the others were already there. They stared up at a hole in the cave's ceiling. It looked big enough for a person to fit through.

"Great. You've found a way out," Gwyn said. She sighed with relief.

"We can't go out," Pango said. "The insects will get us."

"Yes, *you* can," Gwyn said. "I have a plan. I'll need two of your laser lights."

Gwyn took the lights. Then she asked Carlos to push her up through the hole.

Gwyn saw the fireflies outside. They were all around the cave door. She could hear their bodies scraping against each other.

She took out two laser lights. She pointed them into the sky.

Gwyn flashed the lights on and off. She had learned the pattern from the computer. Flash. Flash, flash. Flash. Flash, flash, flash. The signal shot up into space.

On the ground, she heard the sound of beating wings. The fireflies were looking up. Their lights were flashing, too. They repeated the pattern they saw in the sky. One firefly took off. More and more fireflies followed.

"Carlos!" Gwyn screamed. "Lead the crew and survivors back to the spaceship!"

Carlos pulled himself out of the cave. He looked up at the sky. The fireflies were flying up to the signal above them.

Everyone followed him out of the cave. They ran for the spaceship.

Pango was last. He stopped to stand next to Gwyn.

"That was a great plan!" Pango said. "Now let me take over. I'll keep sending the signal."

"No, Pango," Gwyn said. "But thank you. Go prepare the spaceship for **liftoff**."

Pango ran for the spaceship. "Don't wait too long," he shouted.

Gwyn turned her eyes back to the sky. She flashed the lights on and off, on and off.

Suddenly, she felt something pull at her foot. She looked down. A huge, hairy leg was reaching up from inside the cave. There was a firefly inside!

Gwyn felt herself being dragged down. At the same time, she heard the

spaceship's engines start up.

Gwyn looked down into the cave. The insects' two huge eyes were staring at her. Its jaws were moving back and forth.

Gwyn gathered all her strength. Then she punched the insect's leg. For just a second, it let go of her.

That was enough. Gwyn jumped up. She raced for the spaceship. Behind her, she heard the insect trying to get out of the cave.

Ahead of her, the spaceship's door opened. Carlos and Pango pulled her inside. Seconds later, the spaceship blasted off.

Gwyn took a deep breath. Then she walked to the control deck. She sat down in the captain's chair. She stared at the amazing sight outside the spaceship.

Giant fireflies were flying all around them in space. But the insects could not harm them now. Everyone was safe inside the spaceship.

Outside, the fireflies' lights flashed on and off, on and off. Now their lights looked pretty to her. They looked like giant fireworks.

"Mission accomplished," Gwyn whispered to herself.

She set the spaceship's course back home. Back to planet earth.

Do you think Gwyn is a good leader? Why or why not?

Glossary

antennas *(noun)* feelers on the head of a bug

beetle *(noun)* an insect with two pairs of wings

chemical *(noun)* a solid, liquid, or gas that can be mixed with other stuff to form a reaction or make a change

chemical reaction *(noun)* what happens when two or more chemicals are mixed together

crew *(noun)* a team of people who work together on a ship, an airplane, or a job

descend *(verb)* to move down

eerie *(adjective)* strange and scary

flickering *(verb)* turning on and off

insect *(noun)* a bug

laser *(noun)* a strong beam of light

liftoff *(noun)* an upright takeoff by a spaceship

mate *(noun)* the male or female partner of a pair of animals

mission *(noun)* a job

ooze *(noun)* very soft mud

Photinus pyralis *(noun)* the scientific name for a firefly

printout *(noun)* one or more pages of information from the printer of a computer

reflection *(noun)* an image on a shiny surface, such as a mirror *(related word: reflect)*

second-in-command *(noun)* the person who takes over when the leader can't work

slime *(noun)* soft, slippery stuff, like mud

survivors *(noun)* people who live through a disaster or horrible event

tornado *(noun)* a kind of strong storm